XXX BEDTIME STORIES

EXPLICIT DIRTY EROTICA SHORT STORIES

EFRAIN MALLERY, GARRETT ZEIGER,
SHALA BREECE, JULLES MUNSEN, PORTIS
NEWMAN

plicit Press

CHAPTER 1

HUSBAND SCORNED

WHEN I FOUND out that my wife Samantha had cheated on me while on our honeymoon, the only thing I felt was disgust. Gradually as I thought about her half-apology, which followed her confession, another feeling swept through my body. The feeling of the need for revenge. She had walked out of our room, saying that she would leave me alone and let me think. Well, the darkroom didn't quite do me good, and so I'd left for the bar. Maybe a few drinks would help me get through the night.

As I approached the bar, I caught sight of two sexy blonde women talking animatedly and having fun. I sat a few barstools away from where they were and ordered a vodka on the rocks. As I sipped on the drink, I paid hardly paid them any attention. Yes- they were beautiful but I didn't was to get anything started with them. After all, this was how the whole situation had first occurred with my wife. If she remembered that she was married, maybe she wouldn't have cheated on me in the first place.

"Hi...You look lonely, want some company,' a tiny voice from the side of me whispered. It was one of the twins.

They both introduced themselves and walked over to where I had been seating. Their names were Ella and Emma. "We'd love to join you," Ella giggled she was slightly a little more tanned than her sister. However, they both looked similar and it was hard to tell them apart. Thankfully, they were dressed differently and they sounded different in terms of their voices.

I contemplated as to whether I should take her up on her offer. Finally, I said to them, "Why not." The two tipsy women got up from their seats and approached me.

We spent the time chatting animatedly before I invited them back to my room. Maybe it was the alcohol, I wasn't sure. But for some reason, it didn't even matter that Samantha might come back from her little rendezvous at any moment. I sincerely believed that she'd left me to think while she secretly met with her new lover.

As we entered the room, I was suddenly a little conscious as to what I was doing. My eyes searched the darkroom, nervously, hoping that my wife was still out. Thankfully, she was and the three of us were alone. The two women joined me on the bed, kissing and fondling my body. I felt like a prize that they both wanted. While Ella kissed me passionately, her sister busied herself with my bottoms, trying to get them off me. Ella's kisses trailed downwards to my neck, and then my chest. She was slowly undoing the buttons of my top, as she continued her sweet caress.

I took a sharp gasp of air as Emma whipped out my cock and took it into her hungry mouth. Sucking and licking my raw meat, she sent shivers through my entire body. Her tongue worked its way up and down my shaft, building my erection. I groaned as the two women pleasured me beyond my wildest dreams. This would be my very first threesome ever and I hadn't known it would have felt so good. It was just like in the adult movies that I would watch secretly.

"Oh yeah!" I cocked my head back onto the fluffy pillow and closed my eyes, while Ella, who had been focusing on the top part of my body, began caressing my somewhat tender nipples. She was gently tugging and biting them.

Meanwhile, her sister continued sucking on my manhood, increasing the momentum of her sucks as she went along. My body shuddered as tiny spasm shot through me. My cock throbbed in anticipation of penetrating her core. She released my cock from her mouth and got off the bed briefly to undress. As the sheer white dress she'd been wearing dropped down to the floor, her gorgeous petite body was revealed. She had the perkiest breasts I'd ever seen, I wondered if her sister looked just as pretty. Ella then mounted me again, this time in reverse position with her rear end facing me while her head was positioned directly over my cock. As she caressed my cock, her pussy looked more and more inviting from the back. I could tell that she was getting aroused by giving me a blowjob. I slipped my fingers between her moist folds stroking her tender flesh.

Ella moaned out in delirium bucking her pussy against my fingers while her tongue ravished my cock. Meanwhile, her sister, Emma, was fondling my nipples while her hand stroked my body. I drew my fingers out of Ella and realized how wet she was. My fingers glistened with her juices on it.

"Oh my God," I thought to myself. I needed to taste her sweet juices. Taking hold of her hips, I pulled her body closer to my mouth. When my tongue made contact with her moist flesh, she squealed out my name.

A warm feeling coursed through my body as Emma's wet pussy plummeted on my rock-hard cock. She'd left the position where she'd been and moved down the bed, to ride my cock.

Rocking her pussy against my cock, she let out moans of pleasure, while working her wetness up and down my shaft. While she rode my cock, my tongue darted into the slit of Ella's moist pussy, flicking repeatedly at her insides.

Both women seemed to be thoroughly enjoying themselves. And I was enjoying the sensations that they were bringing about. This was definitely double the pleasure. Emma continued to ride my cock increasing the momentum of her movements, slamming hard unto my cock. Her cries were loud and filled with desire as she continued coating my shaft with her juices. Her tightness was being stretched beyond its limits. As our passion intensified, I began heaving my groin area thrusting my cock upwards meeting her downward thrusts halfway. Our movements became one and soon she was summiting her earthshattering climax. Crying out, as she slammed her wet pussy on my cock repeatedly.

Finally, she reached her orgasm and slowly began relaxing onto my cock. After taking a few seconds to catch her breath, she rolled over and called to her sister. Telling her to come to enjoy my cock.

I released Emma's pussy from my mouth and she quickly made her way to my still erect cock. It took everything I had to control myself. I didn't want to ejaculate before fucking both women.

As the other sister pushed her pussy downwards, on my cock a wave of passion rushed through my body. Good God, her pussy felt even warmer than that of the girl before. She was so wet, so tight so sweet. I immediately began heaving my groin upwards, thrusting my cock into her pussy. I groaned out as her sweetness stroked my cock.

Ella, who'd just enjoyed her orgasm minutes before her, came to her side, fondling her nipples in plain view of my lustful eyes. The throbbing in my dick intensified and I increased the momentum of my thrusts. Gripping unto Emma's hips, I held her in position while I gave her several hard relentless thrusts that seemed to send her into another world and space each time.

With closed eyes and a clenched fist, she bucked her pussy into the cock, rocking viciously, until we both cried out in the heat of the moment as we each climaxed and exploded a sea of our juices.

It took us a few minutes to calm down. The two women found themselves in comfortable places next to me, one on each side as we dozed off into deep sleep, tired and spent from our wild erotic adventure.

"WHAT THE HELL IS GOING ON HERE!"

My eyes shot open and caught sight of my wife Samantha standing at the foot of the bed in utter surprise. Her eyes were inflamed with fury and she shook with anger. There was no way I was getting out of this one. I'd been caught!

"GET OUT! GET OUT NOW!" she bellowed causing the other women in the room to awake out of their sleep. The twins quickly got off the bed and scurried into their clothes, leaving the room without even saying goodbye.

I stood there, speechless. Of course, I knew that something like this could happen. I wanted to smile...I had paid her back tenfold.

What would now be the status of our relationship? Perhaps over. But I didn't really care at this point. No woman should cheat on her husband while on their honeymoon. Ahhh...revenge tasted sweet.

CHAPTER 2

THE SISTER

I HAVE BEEN MARRIED for almost two years now. Unfortunately, my wife and I already had our issues in the bedroom. She was great for about the first year. Then she turned cold and distant. Needless to say, I walk around horny with a semi-hard on most of the time. It was getting to where toothless fat girls were becoming a turn-on for me. I wondered how bad it would get before I would be so desperate.

I was not a happy man. I was incredibly horny and now I find out my wife's long-lost sister is coming for a visit. How much worse could it get? Now I would have two estrogen receptacles angry with me. All-day long, my wife bossed me around squawking honey do this and honey do that. One time when she had her head turned, I yanked my semi-woody out and said "Honey do this" and then popped him back in his zippered hiding place.

My wife finally left to go get her darling sister from the airport. She had been in Europe studying for the past two years. She's probably a real bitch, I thought to myself while I feverishly clicked on a Porn Hub episode I could jerk off to real fast. I never could find a hot enough babe on Porn Hub to relieve my strained and hurting woody before I heard the wife and her sidekick pull up. I quickly stuck him back in his cave and X'd out of porn real quick and flipped onto the news page about inflation.

I really wasn't paying much attention when the two of them came in through the side door. I was in the kitchen making myself a sandwich when in walks the hottest little piece of flesh in a tight skirt that I had ever laid eyes on. I am sure my eyes bugged out and I started to drool. I also dropped the cheese I was holding in my hand and it hit the floor. The little bitch giggled at me and usually I'd be pissed, but who the fuck cares. She was made to be devoured by the eyes of perverts like me. She might as well get used to it. If she is going to parade around in a tight mini skirt and a tank top showing off her pointed nipples she may as well be prepared to be openly drooled over.

"Jack, this is my little sister Chastity," said my ball and chain. I didn't even bother to glance her way as I stared at Chastity's hot tits and hugged her close enough to feel my boner through my jeans. She tried to squirm from my grasp but I nonchalantly pinched her bubble butt on the way out of our embrace. She rolled her eyes but she still made sure I saw her panty-less cunt when she bent over to pick up her napkin that she "dropped". I about busted a nut right there on the kitchen floor. I was so tempted to let this boner pop out of my jeans' zipper like a nasty jack off in the box.

This little cunt was shameless. Here she knew she was purposely showing me her pussy with its long chocolate-colored lips, but then she acts appalled. She was such a dirty slut it made me want to fuck her eat her and drench her in my cum.

I had to find a way to get the wife to leave for a while so

I could fuck the brains out of her hotter little sister. Amazingly enough, I didn't have to make the wife do anything. She came into the living room announcing she had to run to the market and to the library to return some videos and get more. I purposely siphoned about half the gas out of her vehicle so hopefully she'd run out and have to get help. I wanted her gone as long as possible. I even explained to her not to pay attention to the gauge. She had plenty of gas left.

She was no longer out of the driveway than I was on my way to visit her little sister's room. I almost fell out when I got to the opened doorway. I peeked inside and there she was butt naked playing with her wet pussy on the bed. I thought I might have to lure her out of her clothes but no way! This little tease was already naked and waiting on me to fuck her brains out. I walked over to her, unzipped my jeans and my dick popped out like a stiff rod and I sunk it down her throat.

She gagged at first but then she opened her greedy throat up wide and took the full length of my shaft down to the gonads. I got my cock to the point I thought I'd unleash my seed down her throat and I pulled out quickly.

I told her horny ass to turn over so I could screw her doggie style. I wanted to bang her good from behind. That is exactly what I did to my naughty little sister-in-law. I watched as her big brown pussy lips engulfed every inch of my wood-hard prick. It felt better and better the harder I pounded her drenched cunt. I could tell she was about to cum all over my horny dick. Her lips groped tighter at the base of my shaft. I knew it was a matter of moments and I'd shoot my dick off inside her hole.

I was right. I knew my cock pretty damn well. In less than a minute later, I was reeling in ecstasy as I had an orgasm and came for what seemed like a solid five minutes inside her unbelievably juicy pussy. I groaned so loud I heard the next-door neighbor's dog starting to howl back at me. That afternoon with her started a series of secret fucks between me and my wife's hot little sister. Who says it isn't fun having family come to stay with you?

CHAPTER 3

THE TUTOR

I HAVE BEEN a certified college algebra/math teacher for about 15 years now and to make a few extra bucks I decided to take on a tutoring job in the summer. I was 40 and recently divorced and feeling depressed in general. It is right what all the books say.

When a woman turns forty she truly starts to feel over the hill, unloved, and downright unattractive. This is why the male student I tutored this summer had such a profound and sexual effect on me.

I checked my email messages one day and saw a message from a young 20-year-old male who was struggling with his college algebra course. I answered the mail and told him I would be more than happy to tutor him on Mondays. I gave him my house address and waited for his response. He responded rather quickly and he agreed to be at my house on Monday at 3 pm. I was happy because I really needed the extra cash.

At three o'clock on the dot the young man, whose name was Jason, showed up at my door. I was impressed by his punctuality among other things. He was smoking hot as well. He was 20 years my junior, but still I was incredibly attracted to him. I will admit as he sat close to me as I explained quadratic equations, I became increasingly more turned on. I caught a glimpse down at his crotch and saw that he was beginning to get a huge boner as well. From my experience, I would guess he was about 8 inches long at least. Also the way the head bulged through his pants I could tell it was huge. Nothing turned me on more about a cock than a huge head on it.

I reached over and nonchalantly touched his knee while I explained the problem we were embroiled in. He looked up at me with curiosity but definite interest in his eyes. That was enough to give me the incentive to push it a step further. I leaned over him and tossed my long red hair in his face. I also gave him a view of my huge 36 DD tits. His eyes about popped out of his head.

That was all it took and before either of us could control our fleshly desires we were involved in a heated French kiss. He damn sure knew how to kiss because every second that passed my cunt grew increasingly more drenched. Jason certainly knew how to turn a lady on. He reached under my skirt and began to fondle my bald cunt. That was my cue to unzip his Levi's and pull out his amazingly massive boner. Fuck! I hadn't had my hands around a dick like this in a month of Sundays.

His head bulged so profusely it was purple and the veins on his large shaft stood out in attention as well. I found myself dropping to my knees and taking his hard-on in my mouth and sucking ferociously. He tasted so damn good. He tasted just like a horny dick should taste. I sucked on Jason's cock for a solid 10 minutes and then I decided it was time he put his boner deep inside my screaming pussy.

"Do you want to fuck me and fuck me hard?" I asked him seductively.

"Fuck yes I do!" replied Jason in a very horny tone of voice almost growling.

We made it to my bedroom undressing each other the whole way. Once on the bed, I was blown away by Jason's assertiveness. He buried his head in my bald cunt and began to eat me out like a fucking pussy eating pro. I can very comfortably say I have never had anyone before or since eat my pussy so well and so ravenously. It was the best cunnilingus I had ever experienced. Little did I know the best part was yet to come. When Jason mounted me I went to heaven and back.

He slid his 8-inch trouser snake in me inch by excruciating inch until I almost screamed in all-out pleasure! The missionary position was hot enough but when he lifted my long legs up by his ears I did enter paradise indeed! I could tell Jason had definitely been fucked and been the one to fuck before. He screwed me with the experience of a 40-year-old man. In fact, he was better than any forty-year-old I had ever been fucked by. I usually avoided being involved with younger men because I didn't think they had the experience to please my greedy snatch, but Jason sure as hell did.

I was about to explode and I longed to cum all over his dick while I rode the fuck out of his big long cock. I asked him if he minded if I screw him on top. He of course said he didn't mind at all. I was ecstatic by this time and I mounted him well. I slipped my bald, drenched cunt down onto his steel pole as slowly as I could possibly stand it. Of course, I wanted to ram my pussy right down on it, but I wanted to tease the two of us first. I did too and I did so very well because when I finally eased down onto that last inch I damn near came then. I think Jason almost did too because I could feel his ball tight up against my asshole. I took him slow and grinding at first and then I started to bounce like nobody's business. It felt so fucking hot being screwed and screwing a big young dick. It didn't take long before he and I were both gushing cream all over my bald cunt and his young lap. I can easily say that Jason was the best fuck this middle-aged MILF had ever had the pleasure of having. I do believe tutoring is the best job for me and I didn't intend to ever stop doing it.

CHAPTER 4

THE WOOD NYMPHO

IT WAS a hot day and the wood nymph had been busy gathering berries and wildflowers to take back home to her cottage. She felt very hot and sweaty so when she came upon the sparkling blue brook she decided to go for a dip. She slowly peeled off her green buttoned-down dress and let it fall loosely on the moss below. She untied her long scarlet mane and let it fall seductively down from her porcelain shoulders. Her whole nubile body was revealed shimmering in the sunlight. From the top of her beautiful head to her coppery muff between her legs the wench looked absolutely delicious and sexy.

She loved the way her pussy hair tickled her white inner thighs. Every time she felt it her fingers could not resist entangling themselves in all that fuzzy hair. She was used to these naughty afternoon swims and felt completely at ease in the setting. She had never been discovered, so she had spent many hours learning how to please the folds between all of that copper pussy hair. She truly was a goddess of the woods, sensual and inviting, with no inhibitions whatsoever. feeling totally natural standing naked beside the small pond.

The wood nympho frolicked and played in the water for a while when she could swear she heard a rustle in the wood. It sounded like crunching leaves underneath shoes. There was something about the water that always seemed to make her hornier. Without the encumbrances of clothes, she was a free spirit that was a vision of loveliness to behold.

She also had a favorite patch of tall grass that she made her bed. After she swam until her body was amply satisfied she usually laid upon the patch of grass with water droplets shimmering all over her skin and she let her body dry naturally in the sunlight. She once again thought she heard a rustle in the wood, so she decided to get out of the water and start drying off.

She lay back with her still wet body glistening in the sunlight. The droplets of water shimmered like diamonds upon her skin. She closed her eyes for a moment to let the sun beat down upon her flesh when surprisingly she looked up to see a handsome man smiling down at her. Typically she would be frightened but something about this man made her feel at ease and very amorous as well. She motioned for the man to join her on her grassy bed. He removed his clothing revealing a very masculine and gorgeous form. This made her only ache for him more. His cock lay by his leg long and semi-hardened and as she looked at it, it grew hard as steel. She took his strong hand and pulled him to her. He pulled one long ivory leg at a time up by his ears and slowly thrust himself inside her greedy cunt. With her legs up by his ears, he could see her pink hairy pussy open up wide looking as though it had been waiting for a cock like his its whole life.

The sexual tension between these two was like nothing

she had ever experienced. Their bodies melded together as if they were made to fuck and make love. He plunged his angry and swollen head inside her with a passion that the wood nymph had never experienced before.

She playfully got up and ran to the pond and dared him to follow behind her. Once in the water, the two of them frolicked like little kids. He'd go underwater and see her long copper pussy hair billowing in the water and try to grab her clit with his mouth. His cock looked like a waving wand of wonder as it moved beneath the gin-clear water. He slid his hand between her legs and watched as his thick fingers disappeared into the copper-haired lips before him.

Up above the water they kissed in motion with their genitals below and her wet snatch felt like a slippery moss-covered rock as he toyed with it. Her lips spread easily as his fingers slid deep inside her. She squatted a bit to drive them deeper inside her demanding cunt. As she pumped against his hand he reached down and squeezed his lanky shaft with his powerful hand. She reached down and pulled his hand away and quickly grasped his throbbing member pulling it to her eager cunt she wrapped a leg around his back and drove his swollen cockhead deep inside her impatient pussy with a single move. Then she groped to find his wet wand that was as hard as granite under the water and guided it deep into her wet muff. Her ass clutched and thrust with a power that even surprised him as her greedy snatch took every inch of his straining cock deeper and deeper into her heated depths. He could feel her inner folds slipping up along his shaft as they fought to grab at his pulsating meat thrusting in and out of her demanding cunt. She slipped her other leg around him and drove her heels into his back forcing every inch of his swollen cock into her slippery pussy. He could feel his balls drawing up as his boiling seed needed to be set free. She too could feel the need for release and began slamming her pussy against his groin making the water splash noisily. His hands slipped down to her ass and yanked her tightly against his crotch. She frantically wiggled from side to side as she rubbed her clit and lips against his coarse cock hair

Her head laid back as she impaled herself on this ready-to-explode cock. Her eyes were wide open one minute and then slammed shut the next as she felt the first convulsions of her pussy

She could feel her cunt grab at his pounding shaft and knew he would soon fill her demanding pussy with his thick hot seed. With a sudden animal growl, he plunged his cock as far as it would go in her cumming cunt. She felt the heated seed of his balls splash against her inner cunt walls amid the coolness of the water.

Her orgasm made her glad he was supporting her as it was so intense she would have collapsed on weakened knees had she been standing on her own. She felt his spurting cock quiet within her now cum drenched cunt. His breathing was deep and labored as he stood there waiting for her next move. She dropped her heels from his back and let her legs fall weakly into the water

CHAPTER 5

TREEHOUSE FUN

THE WOODEN FLOOR creaked and groaned as Sean shifted his weight to his back. "Are you sure that this thing is going to hold us?" he asked Maggie.

She laughed at his worried expression. "Quit being such a wuss. It's fine," Maggie said as she tucked blonde hair behind her ear and kissed Sean's ear.

Sean shivered and forgot about the noisy boards as Maggie licked his ear and sucked on his earlobe. Her deft hands unbuttoned his jeans and slipped inside his underwear. He sighed as Maggie took his cock in her hands and lightly stroked him.

He looked up when her hands disappeared to see her taking off her tank top. Her boobs jiggled and threatened to pop out of her bra as she threw the top aside. Sean reached up and squeezed one of the large orbs. He loved the way she felt in his hand. Her big tits were just one of the many things that attracted him to her.

Maggie giggled and said, "I love the way you love my boobs."

"I can't help it," Sean said. "They're just so big and

beautiful," he told her as she undid the bra and they spilled forth.

The sight of her pink nipples made Sean's mouth water. He wanted to suck on them so bad. He sat up and took one in his mouth, sucking greedily on it. Maggie put her head back and enjoyed the pleasurable sensations Sean's mouth and tongue created. Her pussy began to throb slightly as he switched to her other nipple and did the same thing.

Sean released her nipple and lay back again. His dick had started to get hard and he shimmied out of his jeans so that it wasn't confined.

Maggie saw Sean's excitement and felt her own body respond to the sight of his growing penis. She reached down and took it in her hands again and started working the shaft until it was nicely standing up. Then she bent down and took his dick in her mouth, licking around the head and then sucking.

Sean moaned and laid his head on the floor of the tree-house and let Maggie do her thing. She licked up and down the shaft, kissed his balls, and toyed with them. Then she took him deep and sucked as she drew back. The suction felt incredible to Sean and he thrust his hips up a little in response.

He said, "Maggie, get that pussy over here so I can lick it while you do that."

Maggie obliged by straddling his face and spreading her legs wide. He was treated to an up-close view of her pretty pink pussy. Sean spread her pussy lips wide so he could see her entrance, which was glistening with pussy juice. He made his tongue stiff and thrust it as far as he could inside her cunt.

Maggie gasped as she felt his tongue sweetly invade her pussy. It felt so good and made her even more excited.

She moaned as she went back to sucking his cock. It was throbbing and rock hard. As she licked it and flicked her tongue over the little hole in the tip, Maggie played with his balls.

Sean growled and started running his tongue up and down the inside of Maggie's pussy enjoying the salty-sweet taste of her. When he got to her clit, Sean moved his tongue back and forth over it and Maggie bucked a little. Sean could tell that she would cum soon if he kept doing it and he wanted to give her that pleasure even as she was pleasuring him.

He got a better grip on her pussy lips and licked her clit in earnest. Maggie whimpered in need and her hips moved involuntarily. She couldn't hold still as Sean drove her to the precipice of bliss. Then the first spasms of her orgasm began and Maggie cried out to Sean.

"Oh, Sean! I'm cumming, baby! It's so fucking good. Don't stop," she pleaded.

Sean had no intention of stopping. In fact, he wanted to see how many times he could make her cum. He flicked his tongue faster over the little bud, drawing out her ecstasy. Maggie's orgasm lasted a long time, which pleased Sean.

Maggie sagged a little as her climax subsided. "Sean, that was fantastic," she said.

Sean chuckled. "I'm not done with you, Mags. Get off and roll over on your
back."

Maggie did as he asked, wondering what he had in store for her. His brown
eyes smiled at her as he grinned and lay down beside her. He sucked on her tits again as he slid a hand down her

flat stomach and cupped her pussy. Sean slid a finger inside her slick cunt and sawed back and forth, in and out.

Maggie laid her head back and gave herself up to him. Sean inserted a second finger and Maggie moaned in approval. He pushed in and pulled out slowly several times then began moving faster and faster. Making sure that the heel of his hand kept hitting her clit, Sean finger-fucked her good.

Intense sensations coursed through Maggie as Sean stroked and rubbed her.

She loved that he was a little rough. He was making her so horny again and the contact he was making with her clit and her G-spot was making her crazy with passion.

"Oh, you make me feel so good, Sean. Fuck me. Do it hard," she said. Her blue eyes looked steadily into his.

Sean said, "You want me to fuck you?" Maggie nodded. "Yeah. I need it."

Sean happily complied, stroking hard and faster. Maggie's hips moved to meet his hand and he added a circular motion. Maggie wanted to see what he was doing and propped herself up on her elbows. She watched Sean's arm action, watched his fingers disappear into her cunt over and over, and then she was cumming.

Sean loved the noises she made as she climaxed. She was getting even wetter with her pussy juices and she moved her hips wildly as her orgasm intensified.

Maggie couldn't even call Sean's name. The only thing she could get out was cries of ecstasy. Her orgasm was barely over till Sean was withdrawing his finger and settling himself between her legs and pushing them as wide as they would go.

He licked and sucked her clit, moving his face back and forth quickly. The different pressure on her love button made her horny so quickly that it left Maggie breathless. She grabbed Sean's head and pushed his face harder into her cunt.

Sean licked hard and fast, relishing how much Maggie was turned on. His dick was throbbing and he knew that he was soon going to have to get it inside her or he would come on the floor of the treehouse. But for the time being, he wanted to give her as much pleasure as possible.

Her clit was swollen and pink and tasted so good. He never let up the pressure and soon Maggie was trembling. She threw her head back as she came yet again. This time she grabbed his shoulder and held on for dear life as he took her over the edge. When the climax released its grip on her, Maggie lay back on the floorboards, panting from the exertion.

Sean smacked his lips and smiled at her. "You taste incredible." Maggie laughed. "I'm glad you like my pussy."

"Love it."

Once she recovered a little, Maggie said, "On your back. I want to ride you."

Sean did as she asked. His dick pulsed and jerked. Maggie took it in her mouth and briefly worked his shaft. She found him hard and ready. Carefully, she straddled his hips and guided his cock inside her pussy. She descended as far as she could and then rose up again.

A hiss of pleasure came from between Sean's lips as her tight sheath pulled on his shaft. The feelings she elicited from him were intense and Sean had to control himself. Maggie moved faster, rising and falling above him. Her breasts swung to and fro and Sean reached for them, playing with her nipples.

Maggie rocked on top of Sean. She wanted to feel him cum, to make him feel like he made her feel. He felt incredible and she loved how it felt with him inside her. Sean couldn't hold back any longer. He thrust his hips up as Maggie came down and he started to cum.

"Maggie, oh, baby! Yeah! Oh shit! It's amazing," he said as he was rocked by a hard orgasm.

He shook as it flowed through him, unable to think of anything but what was happening below his waist. Maggie felt his hot cum fill her and reveled in the sensation. Sean grabbed her hips and held her still for a few moments. Then his climax began to ebb and he could think again.

Smiling up into her beautiful face, Sean said, "Maggie, you're incredible."

Maggie lay down on him and kissed him. "You're incredible," she said. Then she laughed. "I told you we'd have fun in the treehouse."

Sean laughed with her. "Yes, you did, and yes, we sure as hell did. We'll have to come back up here sometime for some more fun."

After a little bit, they dressed and left the treehouse. Both of them replayed their time in it and knew they'd always remember all the fun they'd had there.

ABOUT THE AUTHOR

Efrain Mallery is an emerging erotica author of many erotica kinks and sub-genres. Be sure to check out other books and leave a review if this story got you hot!

Visit my blog at Efrain Mallery Blog

Join my newsletter for the exclusive Efrain Mallery Newsletter

Sign up for Free Stories from Xplicit Press Authors

Xplicit Press Author Updates

Like Xplicit Press on Facebook

Follow Xplicit Press on Twitter

Readers: I want to expand a few of the stories to see where the characters can be explored further. If there are any of the stories that you would like to read more about again, I'd love to hear from you!

Keep In Touch
Efrain Mallery
info@efrainmallery.com